# MRS. GOOSE AND THREE-DUCKS

# MRS. GOOSE AND THREE-DUCKS

By

MIRIAM CLARK POTTER

J. B. LIPPINCOTT COMPANY
PHILADELPHIA NEW YORK

Sixteenth Printing

Library of Congress catalog card number 36-21824

*Printed in the United States of America*

To
CONSTANCE
BARBARA AND NEAVE

# CONTENTS

*Here is Mrs. Goose. She lives all by herself, in a funny little house in Animaltown.*

*And here are Mrs. Goose's best friends, Three-Ducks. They do everything all together, just like one duck.*

*Now turn over the page, and the book will begin.*

## Mrs. Goose's Rubbers

One day Mrs. Goose could not find her rubbers. She looked in the same old place in the dark hall closet, and she looked under the bed, and she looked on the back porch; but she could not find them. So she went to Mrs. Pig's house and knocked at the door.

When Mrs. Pig came to see who was knocking, Mrs. Goose said, "Have you seen my rubbers?"

"Of course I haven't seen your rubbers," Mrs. Pig told her. "They wouldn't be over here at *my* house, would they?"

"I don't know," said Mrs. Goose. "I just thought they might be."

Then she went to Mrs. Squirrel's house and knocked at the door.

When Mrs. Squirrel came to let her in, Mrs. Goose said, "I just came to ask if you had seen my rubbers."

Mrs. Squirrel was making a nut patty-pudding. She had flour on her brown nose and on the end of her tail. "No, indeed, I haven't seen your rubbers," she said. "Did you think they were *here?*"

"I didn't know," sighed Mrs. Goose. "I just thought they might be."

Then Mrs. Goose went home. She looked under the stove, she looked up on the clock shelf, she looked in the waste-paper basket, she looked in the ice-box, and then she went out into her little wee garden and *dug;* but she could not find her rubbers.

Just then Mrs. Sheep went by.

"Oh, Mrs. Sheep," called Mrs. Goose, "have you seen my rubbers?"

Mrs. Sheep stopped by the fence. She had a blue sunbonnet on her white woolly head. "Why, no, I haven't seen your rubbers," she said. "Where do you usually keep them?"

"In their same old place in the dark hall

closet," said Mrs. Goose. "But they are not there."

Mrs. Sheep thought for a minute, and then she asked, "Why do you want your rubbers, anyway, Mrs. Goose? The sun is shining."

"Well, it might rain tomorrow," Mrs. Goose told her, "—and then I'd want them."

"That's right," said Mrs. Sheep. "Come to think of it, I don't know where my rubbers are, either! I'd better go home and look them up." And she hurried on.

Still, Mrs. Goose could not find her rubbers. She looked in the teakettle, she looked on the back steps, she looked in the bread-box, she looked under her pillow, and then she got a ladder and climbed up on the roof and stared all around; but her black eyes did not spy them anywhere.

"Dear me, dear me," she sighed, "where can my rubbers be?"

Then she ate her supper and went to bed. Next morning when she woke up, rain was coming down, drip, drip, drip—on the roof. "Oh, it *is* raining today," cried Mrs. Goose, "and I've got to go to market, and I haven't found my rubbers, and I'll get my poor feet all wet!"

She got up and made her bed and ate her breakfast. She had a cup of corn mush, and five pancakes. She dusted her house, and then she just *had* to go to market. The rain was coming down in big bursts and splashes, and there were puddles all over the sidewalks.

"I *must* find my rubbers!" thought Mrs. Goose. And she looked and looked in all the same places, but they did not turn up. "Well," she sighed, "I shall have to go without them, that's what." And she put on her coat and her bonnet, took her big green umbrella from its place in the dark hall closet, and stepped out on her little porch. Then she put the big green umbrella up.

*Plop—plop!* Two big somethings hit her on the head and almost knocked her bonnet off. They fell down on the porch behind her. "What can they be?" thought Mrs. Goose. She turned around and looked at them. They were her rubbers.

"I must have put them inside my umbrella," said Mrs. Goose. "Oh, now I remember! I put them there so they would not be lost. But it would have been a good deal better if I had put them back in their same old place, in the dark hall closet."

Then she put her rubbers on, and went splashing along through the puddles on her way to market.

## The Surprise Party

"I think I'll have a party," said Mrs. Goose to herself, one fine day. "I'll ask Three-Ducks, Mrs. Squirrel, Mrs. Sheep, Mrs. Pop-Rabbit, and Ragtag and Bobtail. Yes, I'll have a party, and this very afternoon."

So she set about sweeping her little house and fixing it up, though it was very neat before that, too.

"I'll have little fat cream cakes for dessert," planned Mrs. Goose to herself, "and good, good cocoa. I'll make some little barley-sugar candies—and what a fine party it will be! I think I'd better give them toast, first, and we'll all sit down at my little table and eat. I'll use my best blue tablecloth. I'll put the cream cakes in my green glass pudding-dish, and just have the barley candies scattered around anywhere."

So she hurried around, setting the table and dusting off the chairs; then she flew into her tiny kitchen to do the cooking.

For two hours she worked there, flapping her wings, shaking her tail, cocking her long goose neck this way and that. She wore a wide blue apron and a baker's cap. She stopped to fan herself now and then, for it was hot in the kitchen.

The morning went along; she dashed to Mr. Gobbler's General Grocery to get pink sugar for the top of her cream cakes; she hopped up to the high shelf of her cupboard to find her best blue teapot. At two o'clock she was all ready, and she said, "Now I'll sit down and rest a bit before I change my dress, for they'll be coming at three."

So Mrs. Goose leaned back in her armchair, and shut her black eyes. She thought, "I'll wake up when the clock strikes half-past two."

But she did not wake up then. The clock struck, and there was Mrs. Goose sleeping, with her black eyes shut tight, her yellow bill wide open, and her cap crooked.

It was twenty-five minutes of three—it was twenty minutes of three—it was a quarter of three—and Mrs. Goose had said, "My guests will be coming at three." How surprised she would be at herself for sleeping like that, so close to the hour! How queer, if her company should come and find her dozing away, in her old spotted dress and sugary blue apron!

Ten minutes of three—and suddenly Mrs. Goose woke up with a start. "Oh, it's late, very late," she said, "and how could I have slept so long? I must rush, rush, to get into my blue and lavender dress, and be ready when they come."

So she flew, to get out of her work clothes, and into her party dress. She brushed her feathers, and stuck her feet into her new red shoes. She hurried fast; the clock struck three, but still she was not ready. Five minutes past three—and Mrs. Goose was dressed, clean handkerchief and all. She turned this way and that before the mirror, and was very proud, because she looked so fixed up.

"Fortunately they are a little late," she said, and sat down in her best chair to rock and fan herself. "Well, everything is all ready, and we'll eat just as soon as they come, for *I'm* hungry."

She went to look at the green glass dish full of cream cakes, all covered with a fresh blue napkin.

It was ten minutes past three; it was quarter past three; it was half past. Mrs. Goose kept looking out of the window to see if she could spy her company coming, but she could not. She opened her front door, and stood there gazing and staring all about, but there was no sign of anybody coming up her little front walk.

Suddenly she saw Three-Ducks coming along, going down to Blue Brook with their umbrellas. She rushed down to meet them.

"Oh, hello," she called to them. "Aren't you coming?"

"Coming where?" asked Three-Ducks, opening their yellow bills wide.

"To my house—to my party—"

"To your house? To your party?" Three-Ducks looked very surprised. "We didn't know about any party."

"Why—didn't I invite you?" asked Mrs. Goose. "Of course I invited you. I asked you —and Mrs. Squirrel—and Mrs. Pop-Rabbit—

and Ragtag and Bobtail—and Mrs. Sheep—didn't I? *Didn't I?*" said Mrs. Goose, blinking and thinking hard.

Three-Ducks stood there and twirled their umbrellas, all alike, and said to her, "You didn't ask *us*. We know that."

Then Mrs. Goose looked very sad. "I don't believe I did," she said. "And I don't believe I asked the others, either. I was so busy getting the party ready that I forgot to ask the company!" She pulled out her handkerchief and began to cry great goosie tears. She looked so sad, standing there crying, that Three-Ducks said, "Do you want us to come, Mrs. Goose? We aren't dressed up, but we'll come just as we are, in our everyday feathers, and we'll run along and ask the others, too, if you want us to. Mrs. Sheep is over there, knitting; Mrs. Squirrel is on her front porch, and Mrs. Pop-Rabbit and Ragtag and Bobtail are jumping in the meadow. Do you still want us to come?"

"Oh, yes, indeed," Mrs. Goose told them, "I want you to come, for I have such a nice party ready. Cream cakes, and good, good cocoa, and barley-sugar candy—and toast—and—"

But Three-Ducks did not hear all she said, for

they were off and away to invite the others, just as soon as she said "cream cakes." They loved cream cakes. And they were very glad to help poor old funny Mrs. Goose, too. In ten minutes and a half they were back again, with Mrs. Sheep, Mrs. Squirrel, Mrs. Pop-Rabbit, Ragtag

and Bobtail, who were all very happy to come, even though they weren't dressed up. "For you look beautiful enough for all of us, Mrs. Goose," they said, "in your new blue and lavender dress and fine red shoes. And what fat, fat cream cakes, and what a wonderful surprise party! For it really is a surprise party, when you come all of a sudden, like this!"

## Mrs. Goose's Bath

One evening Mrs. Goose said to herself, "I think I'll take a nice bath in my little green tub. I don't like water as well as my friends Three-Ducks do; no, indeed. I like better to wipe my feathers off with a damp cloth. But today I am going to take a good, warm bath, and get myself all, all wet."

So she got the little green bathtub off its nail on the wall, and put it in the middle of her kitchen floor. She filled the kettle with water, and put it on the stove. She got out two big soft towels, and a piece of pink soap, and her wrapper and slippers. Then she sat down to read the Animaltown paper. "When the water is warm," said Mrs. Goose to herself, "I will start my bath."

She read a story, and looked at some pictures. Then she suddenly remembered that the water must be warm. She ran over to the stove and, sure enough, the water *was* warm—just right for a bath.

"Now for it!" said Mrs. Goose to herself. She put the towels, and the soap, and her wrapper and slippers on a chair by the tub. Then she thought to herself that she had forgotten to get a wash-cloth.

So she rushed to the little linen cupboard and found a nice blue one, with a little flower embroidered in the corner.

She plopped back to her tub again, and got in, with the wash-cloth and the soap.

"The soap is here, and the wash-cloth is here," she whispered to herself, "but still this does not seem like a bath. I wonder what the matter is?"

She began to rub her feathers with the wash-cloth. "This is a funny bath," she said. "Something is wrong. Soap, wash-cloth, me; soap, wash-cloth, me; yes, we are all here, right in the tub. And yet *still* something is the mat ter."

Just then she heard a quacking outside, and

she knew that Three-Ducks were going by on their way to market.

She jumped out of the tub, and ran over to the window. She stuck her long, funny neck out. "Ho, you!" she called. "Come in here, Three-

Ducks, and tell me what is the matter with my bath! Something seems to be wrong."

Three-Ducks laughed. "You've probably forgotten the soap," they told her.

Mrs. Goose looked around, just to be sure, and then she said, "No, I haven't."

"Then you've forgotten the wash-cloth."

Mrs. Goose looked around again.

"No, I haven't. It is a blue one, with a flower embroidered in the corner."

"Well," said Three-Ducks, "we'll come in and look things over, and see what the matter is." So in they waddled.

There was the little green tub, in the middle of the kitchen floor. There was the wash-cloth, and the towels, and the wrapper, and the soap; and Mrs. Goose, waiting to be washed. And there was the teakettle, sizzling on the stove. "I got into the tub," Mrs. Goose told Three-Ducks, "and tried to take a bath, but nothing happened. Something was missing, but I do not know what."

Three-Ducks began to laugh. "Oh, Mrs. Goose," they said, "we knew that you were funny and forgettery, but we didn't know you were as funny as that!"

"What *is* the matter with my bath?" asked Mrs. Goose.

Three-Ducks were laughing so hard that they could hardly quack the answer. Then they said—"The water, Mrs. Goose! You've forgotten to pour the water into the tub!"

Mrs. Goose blinked her black eyes at the sizzling teakettle. Then she began to laugh, too. "Well, I knew it was something important," she said.

## Easter Hat and Easter Bunny

One morning when Mrs. Goose went to her door she found a little wee pink and blue note under the door-mat. There was a corner sticking out; she laughed to see it. She gave it a little pull; then she opened the tiny envelope. "Now for my glasses, quick," she said, and went to the table to get them and put them on her queer bird nose.

She read the note out loud; it was printed on bright green scratch-paper:

"DEAR MRS. GOOSE,

Will you come to Easter breakfast with us this Saturday, before I take the eggs around?

Your friend;

THE EASTER BUNNY."

"Why, that's lovely," smiled Mrs. Goose. "That's very kind of the Easter Bunny." Then she looked out of her window and saw how the spring was coming, with little banners on the willow trees and little ripples on the pond and little fluffs in the clear blue sky. "Everything is coming alive and looking very pretty and getting fixed up," said Mrs. Goose. "I must have a new hat to wear to Easter Bunny's breakfast!"

So she put her shawl right on, and plop-plopped down to Mr. Gobbler's General Grocery to look around.

Sure enough, there was a row of new spring hats on a shelf behind the apple barrels. Mrs. Goose chose a big black and white and orange one and put it on. There was an old mirror hanging on the wall, and she took a look into that.

"Too big!" said Mrs. Goose, and snatched it off. "Why, I can't see my face at all. Just one eye, peeking out. I don't like this hat, no, no! It looks like a waste-basket."

Then she put on another one, a little flat white hat with a green ribbon around it.

"Too little," sighed Mrs. Goose, turning her head this way and that before the mirror. "Why, I can't see much hat, really; just my big

goosie face staring out. I don't like this one, either. It looks like a sandwich."

So she put the little white hat back on the shelf and tried another one, a yellow hat with a red strawberry on it.

"Why, this is just right," she decided, as pleased as could be. "It's very becoming, too. My feather face shows just enough, and I wonder if that's a real strawberry? It looks like a real strawberry," said Mrs. Goose, taking off the hat.

She took a peck at it. No, it was not a real strawberry, but it was too late to think about that. For Mrs. Goose had swallowed it!

"Oh, dear, oh, dear," she said. "What shall I do? I've eaten the strawberry trimming off my hat!"

Mr. Gobbler was very busy tying up a bag of sugar for Mr. Pig. When he was through with that, he came over to Mrs. Goose.

"Trying on hats, I see," he said.

"Yes," Mrs. Goose told him. "And I like this one, very much. How much is it?"

Mr. Gobbler told her, and then he said, stretching his neck out and looking, very close: "But I thought there was a strawberry on it."

"There was," said Mrs. Goose. "But I ate it. It was just a little mistake."

"Did it taste like a mistake?" Mr. Gobbler asked her. Mrs. Goose did not answer—she only gulped—and then Mr. Gobbler said: "Well, it is just a plain hat now; no strawberry trimming."

"I like it this way," said Mrs. Goose, and she rattled down the money to pay for it and plop-plopped out of the store, shaking her tail.

"And now I must hurry," she said to herself. "Why, I don't believe I know where the Easter Bunny lives! I'll just go over to the Wild Woods and ask Old Lady Owl."

So she hurried along, and there was Old Lady Owl in a tree, with her eyes half shut.

"Good morning," said Mrs. Goose. "I am going to Easter Bunny's Saturday breakfast. Can you tell me where he lives?"

"You, youuuuuuu!" hooted Old Lady Owl, looking very sleepy. "Hole in the woods, back of the hill, three times around and up."

"Oh, I don't understand," said Mrs. Goose. "I can never find him. Won't you please tell me again?"

But Old Lady Owl was fast asleep.

"What shall I do?" sighed Mrs. Goose. "Where shall I find the Easter Bunny?"

"Follow the brook, follow the brook," said a little voice, and there was Wee Field-mouse, who had heard it all, and knew.

"Thank you, thank you," said Mrs. Goose, and she plopped along. Sure enough, the brook turned three times around; then she went up. "This must be the hill," she told herself. "And Old Lady Owl said he lived back of it. Well, I'll just go on." And she marched down the hill.

Just then a little spring wind came along that way. It picked up the edge of Mrs. Goose's shawl and flapped it. It blew off her hat. Mrs. Goose ran after it. It rolled along like a pancake. Every time she caught up with it the wind blew it on again; it was just like a game, and the wind was winning. Finally Mrs. Goose caught up with the runaway hat. She set her foot on it hard to keep it still, and stood looking down at it.

"What good yellow straw," she said to herself. "Really, it looks delicious! I wonder if it tastes like the strawberry?" And she took a nip at it.

"Why, that was very nice," said Mrs. Goose.

"I am hungry from having to hurry on so. I'll just take another bite!"

And before she knew it, Mrs. Goose had eaten her hat up—all, all up! Not even a little widge of straw was left. There she was, bareheaded, going to Easter Bunny's breakfast that windy spring morning.

She plopped along a bit, and then she began to cry. "Oh, it's too bad," she said. "I've eaten my hat. I've had my breakfast. I'm not hungry! So how, how can I go to Easter Bunny's breakfast? Why, why should I go?"

Mrs. Goose plopped up the hill again, thinking how silly she was. She took the wrong turn by the brook, she went round and round the hill and down and up again, till she got all mixed up and tired and cold. Then, suddenly, she heard a little song way off behind the bushes:

"The Easter Bunny comes at night
On very gentle feet;
He holds a basket, safe and tight,
Of some things good to eat;

He walks about the house and ground
On very quiet legs,

And in the morning, all around—
Are eggs, eggs, eggs!"

—and there was the Easter Bunny himself, standing right before her, carrying a little basket, and holding out his paw.

"Why, there you are!" he said. "We thought you might be getting lost. Aren't you coming to breakfast with us?"

"I was coming," said Mrs. Goose, "and I had a new hat to wear—but I ate it. Then I wasn't hungry—and I got lost—and now—" Mrs. Goose stopped to think, and then she said happily, "I've been rushing around so hard that now I'm hungry again! Isn't that fortunate? Only I haven't any new hat to wear."

"Why, never mind," said Easter Bunny. "Mrs. Bunny and I haven't any new hats, either. Do come right this way. I'm so glad to see you."

Mrs. Goose hurried home with him. There was Mrs. Bunny waiting, in a fresh pink dress, with good muffin and porridge smells coming out from the kitchen. There was a little table set with a blue and white cloth and little yellow bowls and plates. There were the Easter eggs, waiting in a shining pile on Easter Bunny's pantry shelf. He gave Mrs. Goose a little basket of them.

"This is a very happy morning," she said, as they ate breakfast. "How very much better this muffin tastes than the strawberry on my hat!"

Then they all laughed, and said "Easter Greeting!" to each other.

## A Walk with Three-Ducks

Three-Ducks were walking along the road one day, when they met Mrs. Goose.

"Hello, there!" they said. "Where are you going?"

"Oh, I don't know," said Mrs. Goose. "Just anywhere."

"Then come along with us," Three-Ducks told her, "because that's just where *we* are going."

So she fell in line behind them. They went along and they went along, and suddenly Mrs. Goose said, "Oh, I've forgotten something!"

"What?" asked Three-Ducks, standing still.

"I must go back," said Mrs. Goose. "Back to my house."

"Why?"

"I forgot to lock my door," said Mrs. Goose. "I always lock it when I go out."

"But you have the key dangling around your neck on a red string," quacked Three-Ducks.

"So I do," said Mrs. Goose, looking surprised. "But I don't think I locked the door with it."

"Well, we think you *did,*" said Three-Ducks, "but if you are sure you want to go back, we will go with you."

"I'm sure," Mrs. Goose told them. "I want to see if that door is locked."

So they paddled back, all four, and when they got to the house, Mrs. Goose put her key into the lock and tried to turn it.

"It *was* locked," she said, "but I'm glad I came back, anyhow. So now we can go on."

After they had gone on a way, she said, "Oh, I have forgotten something! I shall have to go back. I shall have to go back to my house."

"Why?" asked Three-Ducks.

"Because I left the key sticking in the lock!" said Mrs. Goose.

"How silly," said Three-Ducks. "Well, if

you think you have to go back, we'll go with you. But we'll *never* get started on our walk!"

So they paddled back, all four, and when they got to Mrs. Goose's house, sure enough, there was the key sticking out of the lock, with the red string dangling down. Mrs. Goose took it out and put it around her long neck again.

"Now we are ready to go walking," she said.

They plogged along, through the green grass and the dandelions, and they got way down to Blue Brook. Suddenly Mrs. Goose said, "Oh, I am very sorry, but I shall have to go back *again!* Back to my house! I have forgotten something else!"

"What, this time?" asked Three-Ducks, feeling very much put out, and waggling their tails.

"I always leave the key under the door-mat," said Mrs. Goose, "and here it is, around my neck, instead!"

"Does that matter?" asked Three-Ducks. "Does it *have* to be under the door-mat?"

"Yes," said Mrs. Goose, "that is its real place, and I always put things in their real places, ever since I lost my rubbers and could not find them."

"Well, we'll go back with you, if you *must*

go back," said Three-Ducks, "but this must be the last time. We'll never get started on our walk!"

So they paddled way back, and Mrs. Goose took the key with the red string off her neck and put it under the door-mat in front of her little door.

"Now we're ready!" said she. "We'll go on a fine walk."

They paddled down to Blue Brook again, and were marching along very happily through the cress and the drippy wet grass, when suddenly Mrs. Goose stopped and said, "Oh, I am very, very sorry, Three-Ducks, but I shall have to go way back again. Way back to my house."

"And why now?" asked Three-Ducks, flashing their black eyes.

"I am so afraid that I left the red string sticking out from under the door-mat," Mrs. Goose told them. "Some one might see it, and pull the key out and open my front door, and gobble my lunch up. I am very sorry, but I shall have to go back."

"Then go along," said Three-Ducks, "because this time we shall not budge a step with you."

"Well, I'll paddle back and see, and then catch up with you," said Mrs. Goose. "And *then* we'll have our walk."

So she paddled back, and the red string was *not* sticking out from under the door-mat; everything was all right.

She hurried, hurried back to find Three-Ducks again, walking down by Blue Brook.

But they were not there. They were way off, out of sight.

For they simply could not wait for such an old fussbudget as she.

## A Fire in the Kitchen

Now, Mrs. Goose was sweeping her little house one morning, and she thought, "I like my home very much. It is cozy and cute; it is just right."

She bent her neck over to pick up a match with her long bill, and she thought, "How awful if my little house should burn up!"

She got to thinking about it, more and more. "Why, if a fire got started, it would burn up my best rocking-chair, and my wooden soup bowls, and my blue and lavender dress, and my pictures, and all my things, and I shouldn't have any house, or anything, or any place to go!"

And she got to feeling so badly about it that she sat down in a chair and cried great, goosie tears, and began to dab her eyes with her apron.

After a while she said to herself, "Oh, mercy me, I've got all hot, crying. I think I'll go out into the kitchen and make myself some lemonade." So she did; a great, big pitcher of cold lemonade. But she still thought about how awful it would be if her home should burn up.

Now, over in her house, Mrs. Squirrel had made herself a nice, new red dress. She had just finished putting in the last stitches. It was a fine dress, with ruffles and puffles, and a bow over her tail. Mrs. Squirrel was so pleased with it that she turned this way and that way before the mirror. Her little boy squirrel, Billy, was not at home to admire her, so she said to herself, "I think I'll run over to Mrs. Goose's, and show her my dress"—and over she ran.

She skipped along, feeling like a red geranium flower loose in the wind. She scuttle-scrattled up on Mrs. Goose's back porch, and opened the little door.

Now, Mrs. Goose had just finished making the lemonade, and she was still thinking about fire. "How awful it would be," she was saying to herself, "if a fire should start right here in my kitchen—" and then she heard the little scrattling, crackling sound that Mrs. Squirrel's toenails made on the back porch, and she thought—"Oh! That must be a fire, right now—I *hear*

it!" and then she looked, and saw Mrs. Squirrel's bright red dress, and she thought, "It *is* a fire—I *see* it—" and she threw the pitcher of cold lemonade right over Mrs. Squirrel and her fine new outfit!

Mrs. Squirrel blinked her eyes and shook herself, and the lemonade ran all over the floor in little rivers. It was very surprising to have a great pitcher of cold wet stuff thrown at you; she sneezed, and felt very angry. She chattered at Mrs. Goose, loud, blustery squirrel talk. "Why did you do that, Mrs. Goose? *What* a thing to do! The idea—pitching lemonade all over your company! And you spoiled my nice new dress. I was coming over to show it to you! You've got it all wet and drippy—and my feet are standing in puddles—and I think there's a lemon seed in my eye! Oh! You crazy, Mrs. Goose!"

Now, Mrs. Goose had felt very ashamed the minute she found out that it was not fire. She said, very softly, "I am so sorry. I was thinking about having my house burn up, and how awful that would be; and when I saw you—all red—I thought—it *was* a fire."

"My goodness, so *that* was it!" said Mrs. Squirrel. "Oh, how silly and funny you are, Mrs. Goose!"

"Take off your dress," said Mrs. Goose, anxious to make things right. "I'll wash it and iron it—and we'll have a snack of lunch together, and I'll try not to make such a bad mistake again."

So Mrs. Squirrel took off her new, sopping-wet red dress, and put on a big old green wrapper of Mrs. Goose's; and they flew around and got out the little tub and rinsed the dress and hung it on the line to dry. As it blew brightly in the breeze, Mrs. Goose looked at it through the window, and said to Mrs. Squirrel:

"I am saying to myself, 'That is not a fire. Don't be excited. Don't be silly. Don't worry,'—what else had I better say to myself, Mrs. Squirrel?"

"Don't be frightened over *nothing,*" said Mrs. Squirrel. "And don't throw before you *look.*"

"Thank you," said Mrs. Goose. "Yes, I'll say those things to myself."

Very soon they sat down to eat, and Mrs. Squirrel said:

"Well, Mrs. Goose, this is a nice good lunch. I love muffins and green salad, and you are being very, very kind to me."

"If I hadn't been so crazy, we might have had lemonade, too," said Mrs. Goose. And then they both laughed.

## The Lost Apron Pocket

One day, Mrs. Goose said to herself, "I think I'll make myself a nice blue apron. I need a new one very much."

So she took her funny hat with the curly feather on it, and went to Mr. Gobbler's General Grocery to buy some cloth.

She came plop-plopping up to the counter, and told him what she wanted: "Some blue checked stuff to make an apron." Mr. Gobbler showed her a nice piece, and Mrs. Goose said, "I'll take that much, please," and measured, with her wings spread out so-wide.

Mr. Gobbler cut it off with a pair of scissors

that went snip-snap CUT, snip-snap CUT, wrapped it up in some bright green paper, and gave it to Mrs. Goose. She was very happy, plop-plopping home with her bundle; and when she got inside her funny little house, she took off her hat and sat down at her table with needle, scissors, and thread. She cut and then she sewed. She worked very hard, and for a long time. Once in a while she yawned. Mrs. Goose looked very funny yawning, with her bill open wide.

She noticed that she had a little scrip-scrap left, and she said to herself, "Why, I can have a little pocket on my apron!" She was very happy about this, and quite proud when it was done. It was very neatly sewed, just as nice on the wrong side as on the right.

She put her new blue apron right on, and fixed up her room. It was all in order when there came a knock at the door.

Mrs. Goose said to herself, "Company!" She gave her apron a little pat to be sure it looked all right. Then she went plodder-plodder-plunk to the door.

There stood Mr. Pig. He had come to call

on his old friend, Mrs. Goose. He looked very fine, with a new red jacket on.

"Do come in, Mr. Pig," said Mrs. Goose, being a polite hostess. "Won't you sit down? And I'll make us a cup of tea and a sandwich."

That was just what Mr. Pig had hoped, for he LOVED to eat. So he sat down, saying in a pleased, grunty voice, "Thank you, Mrs. Goose. Very nice, very nice."

Mrs. Goose scurried around and made the tea and sandwiches. She made twelve sandwiches; Mr. Pig ate nine of them. Then he said, "And now I must be going. Thank you for the pleasant little nibble."

"Nine sandwiches is more than a nibble," thought Mrs. Goose to herself, as she began to wash the cups and saucers. "I'm glad I don't gobble the way pigs do. Well, I'm very glad I was dressed up so nice and clean, in my new apron, all ready for company." She looked down at herself, smiling a proud goosie smile. Then she was astonished. For there was no pocket.

No, the apron was just plain. No pocket at all. Mrs. Goose did not like that. She had planned to carry peppermints and money in that pocket. "I'll run and take a look in the mirror—" she said to herself. "Maybe my eyes don't see right."

So she ran to her bureau and stared. But no, she saw no apron pocket in her mirror.

"What could have become of it?" she thought. "Where is my pocket?" And she put on her glasses, and looked again.

"Well," she said, taking off her glasses and putting them away, "I made a pocket, and sewed it on. And I can't see it with my glasses, or with my plain black eyes. I can't see it in the mirror, when I stand right before it and stare. I'll go out and look down the well. Really, one sees very clearly in the water." So out she ran.

Now, Mrs. Goose's well was an old, old one. It had a bucket on a sweep, just like a pussy-in-the-well picture in a nursery rhyme book. Mrs. Goose jumped up on the stones around the well and looked down. There were her head and long neck, looking up at her from the water.

"But I can't see my apron very well!" said Mrs. Goose. She leaned farther over, and SPLASH—she fell in. Way down into the well, right into the cold water.

Mrs. Goose paddled around on the top of the

water, kicking and spluttering. She thought, "Now I am in a fix. Here I am, in this cold, dark place. No one will ever find me." Then, "Help! Get me out!" called Mrs. Goose. But no one heard her.

* * * * * * *

After a long while, Three-Ducks came along that way. They stopped with a jerk, all together, and said, "Let's go in and see Mrs. Goose a bit. The door's open; she must be somewhere about." So they sat down in three chairs to wait for her.

"It is very funny," they said, after they had waited awhile, "that she doesn't come. Something must have happened to her."

They went out the door, and there was Mr. Pig going by to Mr. Gobbler's Grocery, planning to buy cabbages for his supper. "Hello, Mr. Pig," they quacked. "Have you seen Mrs. Goose?"

"Why, yes," Mr. Pig told them. "I went to see her this very afternoon. I had a bite of tea there."

"Well, she isn't here," said Three-Ducks, "and her house is open, too, just as though she were about. But she isn't about, Mr. Pig. Where do you think she is?"

"Hmmmmm! That's very funny," grunted Mr. Pig. "Here comes the Black Cat from Green Street. We'll just ask him if he knows where Mrs. Goose is."

But the Black Cat said no, that he hadn't seen Mrs. Goose. It was very queer that her house was open and she was not there—very queer indeed.

There was a whirr of wings. There was Old Lady Owl from the Wild Woods. "I saw you all here, in a sort of commotion," she said. "I saw you from my tall tree. What's up? What's the matter?"

"She's missing," said Three-Ducks.

"Whoooooooo?" hooted Old Lady Owl.

"Why, Mrs. Goose, of course," said the Black Cat from Green Street.

"She's been gone a long time now," grunted Mr. Pig. "We're afraid something has happened to her."

"We'd better go into her house and look around again," said Black Cat.

So they all went in.

"Here are some dishes, half washed," said Old Lady Owl. "Yes, I'm afraid something has happened to her. She's in some sort of trouble somewhere. Let's open her bed up, and put her slippers out. Let's get some water from the well and heat it; she may be cold or tired or sort of banged-up when she gets back. She'll want a bath and a nap."

They all thought that Old Lady Owl was very wise indeed. Three-Ducks went to fix the bed, all pulling at the red and white quilt together, with their yellow bills. The Black Cat from Green Street put the long gray nightgown on the bed, and the slippers, too. Old Lady Owl ran to poke up the fire in the stove. And Mr. Pig said, "Now let's go out and get some water."

They ran out, and let the bucket down the well.

The Black Cat began to pull it up. "It's VERY heavy," he said. "Of course, it's quite a big bucket—but—"

"I'll help you," said Mr. Pig. So they pulled together. Then POP, up flew the bucket, with Mrs. Goose in it. Her long neck stretched out, and the water drip-dripped all around, as she sailed up through the air.

How surprising, to pull Mrs. Goose from the well! They all looked up and stared.

"Hello," she said. "I was in an awful fix. I was just leaning down to look at myself—and I fell in."

"Just looking at yourself?" asked Three-Ducks. "Why did you lean over so far?"

"I've forgotten why—" said Mrs. Goose. "But I'm sure I had a very good reason."

They all looked at each other, as if they wanted to say, "Isn't Mrs. Goose funny?" And then they told her, "Now come in and take your soppy duds off. Then you must have a hot bath."

"Not a bath!" said Mrs. Goose. "I've had too much water already!"

"Then you must go to bed and get warm," Old Lady Owl told her firmly. "I nevei heard of such a thing—spending a whole afternoon splashing around in a well."

They all hurried into Mrs. Goose's house. A little river of water ran along behind Mrs. Goose. She shook her tail, and drops spattered in all directions.

Old Lady Owl took off Mrs. Goose's apron, and shook it.

"Oh, now I remember why I was looking in the well!" said Mrs. Goose. "I made that apron this afternoon, and I put a pocket in it. Mr. Pig came for tea. After he went, I looked at the apron, and there was no pocket in it! Do you think it could have dropped off?"

"Certainly not," said Old Lady Owl. "Maybe you put your apron on wrong side out, and the pocket was on the other side." She turned the sopping thing over, and there was the pocket, just as she had thought.

Poor old funny Mrs. Goose! They all wanted to laugh at her, but she looked so bedraggled and sad standing there, wet as sops, with her tail hanging down, that they just said, "Now, put on your gray nightgown, and we'll make you a cup of hot tea."

"And do have some with me," said Mrs. Goose, being a polite hostess again. "I'm sorry there aren't any more sandwiches." (She looked at Mr. Pig.)

They wrapped her up in a blanket, and then they all had tea and carrots, as soon as Three-Ducks hung the wet apron out on the line.

It flapped in the breeze, flippery floppery, and sprinkled raindrops on the grass below.

## MRS. GOOSE'S GARDEN

It was warm, sunny weather, and the Animaltown people were digging and planting in their little yards. As she watched them, all busy with their hoes and shovels, Mrs. Goose said to herself, "I love onions. I wish I had a garden all full of them. That's what I'd like."

She was eating onions when she said this, at her table in her little funny house.

"I must plant a great many onions," she kept saying to herself. "A whole garden full of them."

So she went right to Mr. Gobbler's Grocery, and bought a package of onion seeds. She planted them and she planted them, all around in her little garden.

That afternoon, she went out to see if they had come up yet.

No, they weren't up. Of course they weren't.

This made her a little cross and disappointed. She walked up and down in her little garden, talking.

"What are you looking for, Mrs. Goose?" asked Mrs. Squirrel, who was going by on her way to town.

"I'm looking to see if my onion seeds are up yet," said Mrs. Goose.

"When did you plant them?"

"This very morning."

"Then of course they aren't up!" Mrs. Squirrel told her. "They couldn't be up so soon! You must wait awhile."

Mrs. Goose sighed, and said, "All right."

So she sewed a long seam on a sheet she was making, and then she said, "Now I've waited quite awhile. I'll just go out and see if my onions are up yet."

But they were not, of course.

Then she saw Mr. Pig coming by.

"Come and see what is the matter with my garden," she asked him.

Mr. Pig came and looked. "I don't see any garden," he said.

"It is coming," Mrs. Goose told him. "I planted the seeds this very morning. Good onion seeds. But they aren't up."

"Of course not," said Mr. Pig. "You must wait. And when they are up, are you going to have some good—er—creamed onions, Mrs. Goose?"

Mrs. Goose did not like to have Mr. Pig hint about eating up her onions, so she just said, "I don't know," and went quickly back into her house.

She began to read a book about nice gardens. After a while she looked at the clock. "Mercy me," she said. "It is half-past two. Well, if my onions are not up by quarter of three, I'll ring a bell—that's what I'll do. *That* will get them up!"

At quarter of three she went out of her house again. She stared at all the places she had planted the seeds. But nothing was there, no little green things.

So she dashed back into her little house, and

got her big bell. She rang it and rang it, all around her garden.

But nothing happened.

Mrs. Goose put the bell back on its shelf, and sat down in her rocking-chair. "If they are not

up at four," she said, "I shall cry. I shall be very patient till four."

So she got out her knitting, and knitted and knitted till the clock struck. Then she went out into her garden.

"Oh, I don't see what's the matter with them!" wailed Mrs. Goose. "They've had plenty of time. I'll just go out and have another look—" And she walked all around her little garden, staring at the ground, turning her long neck this way and that, and making little pecks at the soft soil.

There came Mrs. Squirrel, on her way back from town. "What's the matter, Mrs. Goose?" she asked. "Are you still looking for your onions?"

"Yes," said Mrs. Goose. "They are so slow."

"You mustn't watch," Mrs. Squirrel told her, setting down her little blue market basket. "It takes a long while for seeds to grow. Do something else. Be busy."

"Well, then," said Mrs. Goose, "I shall clean up my house."

So she got out her soap and brushes, did herself up in her big blue apron, and set to work. She scrubbed and she cleaned and she scoured. She washed all her dishes and all her pots and pans, and she popped her clothes and her curtains into the tub and washed them, too. She spent days doing this.

One afternoon she said, "Oh, my blankets. I

must air my blankets out on the line. I forgot that."

So she strung out a long clothes-line, and as she was pinning the things up, she said, "What are all these funny little green things poking through the ground? See, I am stepping on them."

Mrs. Squirrel was sitting on her little porch, and Mrs. Goose called to her, "Come and see the new grass I have got."

Mrs. Squirrel came skittering over. She stared at the green things. Then she said, "Grass? I thought you were expecting onions."

"Why, so I was." Mrs. Goose was very pleased. "That's what these little green things are—onions. How quickly they came up!"

And that's how Mrs. Goose got her garden.

MUSIC FOR THE DANCE

One day Mrs. Goose felt very gay. "I think I'll have another party. This time it is going to be a dance. We'll all dance—" she planned to herself, happily.

"Yes," went on Mrs. Goose, looking around her little room, "we'll set the table and the chairs around the walls. That will leave a nice clear place in the middle. Then we can hop and jump and dance, and have a happy time of it."

Mrs. Goose was very glad, planning for her party. "We'll have things to eat," she said, "nice cakes—piles of them." She set to work at once, making the cakes. When they were finished, she ran out to ask her company. "I am not going to forget that, this time," she told herself. "That shows what an old silly-nilly I am—once I forgot to ask my guests! But this time it's going to be all right—" and she laughed soft bird laughter to herself.

She plop-plopped down the little street toward Animaltown, and saw Three-Ducks, sitting all in a row on a bench.

Yes, they said they would just love to come to her dancing-party. "But we don't think we are very graceful dancers," said Three-Ducks, looking at their feet. "Just let us march around, in time to the music."

"Do anything you like," said Mrs. Goose, smiling a goosie smile, "but don't forget to come." Then she asked Mr. Pig.

He said he was too fat to dance, but he would come anyway. "For I suppose you'll have—er—refreshments—won't you, Mrs. Goose?" asked Mr. Pig.

"Of course," Mrs. Goose told him, snapping a black eye. She went along and asked Mrs. Squirrel and Mr. and Mrs. Pop-Rabbit, and then she remembered Mr. Gobbler, down at the Grocery, and asked him, too. She stopped at the little queer house of the Black Cat, on Green Street. They were all very happy to come. They said they felt just like dancing.

Mrs. Goose ran down to the brook and picked some violets. She put them in little jugs and bottles all around, even on top of the stove and in the sink. "Now my house looks very pretty," she told herself. "The good refreshments are all ready, the table is all set, the flowers are all picked and put around; the room is cleared out for dancing. We can just dance and dance and dance—everything is all fixed and waiting."

When the hour for the party came, Mrs. Goose was all ready, in her blue and lavender dress. The first to come was Mr. Pig.

He had on a pair of big blue and white striped trousers; his red necktie was an enormous thing, as thick as a towel. He stamped in and took the best chair. Then he smiled happily and said, "I'm all ready for the dance, Mrs. Goose. I am not too fat, after all." And then he whispered, "I'm hungry already!"

Then came Three-Ducks. They had strings of red berries around their white necks. They sat down and admired the violets, though they thought it was very funny to see them on the stove and in the sink.

Mrs. Squirrel came running in, in a brown dress, with her tail tied up in a red bow. And Mr. and Mrs. Pop-Rabbit, with new rabbit shoes on, just right for dancing. They had new gloves on, too, tiny and tight.

Mr. Gobbler wore a white collar, and a big green bow. He had black stockings over his bird feet. "They make nice, soft dancing—black stockings," said Mr. Gobbler.

But where was the Black Cat from Green Street? There he came—sliding along in a bright orange jacket.

"And now, Mrs. Goose," said Mrs. Squirrel, "here we are, all ready for the dancing. How very nice of you to think of giving a party, and such a good one, too."

"All right—start the music," grunted Mr. Pig. "Where *is* the music, Mrs. Goose? I don't see any piano or violin or horn or organ or little music-box around anywhere."

"Perhaps the music hasn't come yet," whispered Mr. and Mrs. Pop-Rabbit politely.

"It will probably be here in a minute," said Mr. Gobbler.

"It's early yet—it will come soon," said Mrs. Squirrel.

*"We* believe Mrs. Goose forgot the music," said Three-Ducks.

And there was Mrs. Goose standing in the middle of the floor with her bill wide open, looking so funny and scared. Yes, it was true; she *had* forgotten the music. They could tell that by looking at her. She was ready to cry. There—the tears came, great, big goosie tears—drop, drop, drop down from her bill, and splash, splash, splash down the front of her blue and lavender dress.

"Here, take my handkerchief," said Mrs. Pop-Rabbit, and she kindly wiped away Mrs. Goose's tears.

"Oh, oh, oh—I forgot the music!" wailed Mrs. Goose. "I remembered everything else—but I did forget the music. Oh, dear, oh, dear—what shall we do? How can we dance without it?"

"I'll try grunting for you," said Mr. Pig. "Ugh, ugh, ugh, just like that—one, two, three—"

"All right," said all the guests, trying to be

happy, because they were so sorry for Mrs. Goose.

So Mr. Pig grunted the best he could—but it didn't sound pretty, a bit. No one wanted to dance to such crazy music.

Then Three-Ducks tried quacking—but that was no better.

"Oh," wailed Mrs. Goose, "my party is all spoiled! How can it be a dancing-party when we can't dance?"

"What kind of music were you going to have, Mrs. Goose?" her friends asked her.

"Why, I was going to ask Mr. Groundhog to come over with his mouth-organ. He plays so nicely."

"Oh, that would have been just too fine for anything," said all the company at the party, a little sadly.

"He's gone to bed now," said Three-Ducks. "He always goes to bed at five."

"I know," said Mrs. Squirrel, with her round brown eyes shining, "but let's go and wake him up. Maybe he will come and play now. It's just over the hill a bit; let's go over and ask him."

"That's a good idea," said Mrs. Goose and all the party. So they put out the candle and locked the door, and all trooped off across the hill to Mr. Groundhog's.

His little door was shut tight. He was sleeping so soundly that he didn't hear them knocking and scratching and saying: "Mr. Groundhog, wake up, please." Then Mr. Pig made a

great BANG, and Three-Ducks gave three tremendous quacks—and the door flew open.

"Hello—who's there?" asked Mr. Groundhog, blinking.

"It's just Mrs. Goose and her party. We wanted some music to dance by. Mr. Groundhog, wake up and bring your mouth-organ—and play us some nice tunes."

"Too sleepy!" yawned Mr. Groundhog.

"But we have some fine refreshments," said Mrs. Goose. "Strawberry lemonade, and piles of cakes—"

"Piles?" asked Mr. Groundhog.

"Yes, just piles!"

"What kind are they?"

"Honey and chocolate, and sweet wild plum."

Mr. Groundhog made a sleepy noise. Then he made a hungry grunt. "All right, I'll come," he said. "If I won't have to dress. If I can just bundle up in my big blanket."

They said yes, that of course he might; so he came stumbling out all done up in his big red blanket, holding the organ in his brown paw.

Then they all went trooping back to Mrs.

Goose's house. And Mr. Groundhog sat in the best rocker, and played such lovely wheezy music, all full of trills and squeaks and little ups and downs. He played *The Stars Are Out To-night* and *The Animaltown March* and *Quack-Quack and Moo-Moo*—all tunes that he had made up.

And how the party danced! Three-Ducks danced all together, in a big feather bunch; Mrs. Squirrel danced with Mr. Pig, and Mr. and Mrs. Pop-Rabbit whirled around together. Mr. Gobbler danced with Mrs. Goose, and he kept telling her how very nicely she put her feet up and down, and what a fine party it was. Black Cat danced by himself—a sort of a chase-your-tail dance in the dark corner, but he had a very good time at it.

After a while they all had refreshments: strawberry lemonade, and just piles of cakes. Mrs. Goose put seven cakes on a plate for Mr. Groundhog, and he ate them all up. He was so tired from playing that he was very hungry. He had one more cake than Mr. Pig, for Mr. Pig had only six.

They all said, when they went home, that they would never, never forget Mrs. Goose's dancing-party, which began so badly and ended so well. And then they took Mr. Groundhog home and put him to bed, all bundled up in his blanket.

## Mrs. Goose and Little Duck

Mrs. Goose had just finished making her bed and sweeping her floor when suddenly she stopped and said to herself: "I think I will go over and see my friend Mrs. Duck-over-the-Hill." So she put on her hat trimmed with parsley, and started right off.

"Now for a nice long walk," said Mrs. Goose, as she stepped down from her little porch.

It was a bright summer day, and she went on and on. Past Mrs. Rabbit's house on Whisker Avenue, past Mr. Gobbler's Grocery, way to the little road that led through the Wild Woods, walked Mrs. Goose. Old Lady Owl was in the woods, napping in the top of a plum tree.

"Where are you going, youuuu?" she said, when she saw Mrs. Goose going by.

"I'm going to see my friend Mrs. Duck-over-the-Hill," said Mrs. Goose.

"You're all alone—take me, tooo," said Old Lady Owl.

"I don't mind going alone," said Mrs. Goose, a little snappily. "But I'll take you, if you'll hurry. Will you hurry?"

"No; shoooooo!" hooted Old Lady Owl, and went to sleep again.

Mrs. Goose had gone on a little way when she met the Black Cat from Green Street.

"What are you doing all alone in these woods?" asked Black Cat.

"I'm going on a little visit," said Mrs. Goose. "What are you doing?"

"Just picking catnip," said Black Cat. "Shall I come with you?"

"Not unless you want to," Mrs. Goose told him. "I know my way in these woods."

"Well, I don't want to, very much," said Black Cat, and went on picking catnip.

Mrs. Goose plopped on, across a little sunny

meadow. Butterflies flew over her head; the flowers were full of bees. "Lots of butterflies, lots of bees, but just one goose," said Mrs. Goose to herself. "Maybe I *am* a little lonesome. I should have taken Old Lady Owl with me, or just insisted on the Black Cat's coming." She took the path that went up, then she took the path that went down, and suddenly there was Mrs. Duck's little grass house at the edge of the green pool. Mrs. Duck was swimming in the water, and behind her swam ten little ducks, all kicking their feet very fast.

"Quack, quack, quack, how do you do?" said Mrs. Duck, when she saw Mrs. Goose. "Have you come to see me?"

"I have," said Mrs. Goose. "Are you at home?"

"Of course I am at home," Mrs. Duck told her. "I will come right out of the water. How do you like my new children?"

"They are nice," said Mrs. Goose, looking hard at the little ducks, who were all shaking their little yellow selves in the sunshine.

"Nice, yes," said Mrs. Duck. "But they are lots of work, and lots of bother, and they are always getting into mischief."

"Peep, peep," said the little ducks, speaking happily all together.

Then a thought came into Mrs. Goose's white feather head. "You have so many children," she said. "Ten is too many for one mother. Please give me one, Mrs. Duck. I walked over here all alone, and if I had a little duck I should not have to go back by myself. It would be company for me to have him, peeping around at things."

Mrs. Duck looked at her children, standing there all in a row. "Ten *is* a good many," she said. "They have been very naughty this morning, and I have to scramble to get food for them. Yes, you may have one, Mrs. Goose. Which one do you want?"

"I'll take this one, please," said Mrs. Goose, pointing to the one nearest her.

"Peep, peep, peep," said Little Duck.

"That means he wants to go," said his mother. "He says he will go with you."

"All right," said Mrs. Goose. "We'll start right home."

"But I thought you came to see me," said Mrs. Duck.

"I *have* seen you," Mrs. Goose told her. "I

must go back now. I want to take my little duckie with me."

"Good-by, then," said Mrs. Duck. "Good-by, Duckie," and she gave him a peck-kiss on his tail.

"Peep, peep," said the little thing, and followed Mrs. Goose away.

When they had walked for a while, Little Duck began to peep again; but this time sadly.

"What's the matter?" asked Mrs. Goose, turning around to look at him.

He just kept on making his unhappy little noise, and Mrs. Goose said to herself: "He's hungry, *that's* what. I'll pick him some wild strawberries."

So she did that; but he would not eat them. He only shut his eyes, and stood still.

"He's tired and sleepy," decided Mrs. Goose. "I'll carry him." So she picked him up and tucked him under her wing; but the loud peeping sound came out through her feathers, every step of the way.

"I wish he'd stop," said Mrs. Goose. "There; be quiet, little Peep-Peep; you are going home."

But he kept on peeping, past Mr. Gobbler's Grocery, past Mrs. Rabbit's house, along the street of Animaltown. Mrs. Squirrel was out on her porch, washing her neat little steps.

"What have you got there?" she asked, when she heard the peeping.

"Just a little duck," Mrs. Goose told her. "He's going to live with me."

"He sounds very sad," Mrs. Squirrel said. "What's the matter with him?"

"Just hungry," said Mrs. Goose, and she hurried into her house and set Little Duck on the table.

"In a minute you shall have some bread and milk," she told him; and when it was ready she set it before him in a blue bowl and tied a napkin-bib around his neck.

"Peep—peeeep!" cried Little Duck.

"There, I'll feed you," said Mrs. Goose. But he would not eat. Instead, he jumped down and began to run around the room; under the table, across the corners, over the hearth-rug. Mrs. Goose tried to catch him; she was distracted. He peeped sadly and louder than ever. "Well, I'll put him to bed," said Mrs. Goose. "I haven't tried *that* yet." So she fixed up a bed in a box, with a little pillow and a scrap of blanket. Little Duck was standing under the table; he had stopped peeping by that time and was only looking sad.

"Come to bed," said Mrs. Goose; and she popped him under the blanket. But he jumped up and ran and hid under the stove—and just then there was a tapping at the door.

There stood Mrs. Duck-from-over-the-Hill.

"Peep, peeep," said Little Duck, running to his mother very fast.

"Yes, here I am," said Mrs. Duck. "I wanted my child after all. Nine children seems too few;

ten is just right. Will you give him back, Mrs. Goose?"

"Yes," said Mrs. Goose. "He was not very happy with me. He peeped all the time. He would not eat and he would not sleep and he would not stop running around crying. I think I should be better off alone—and he was homesick for you. Yes, you may have him back."

"Well, good-by, then," said Mrs. Duck-from-over-the-Hill. "I must hurry back to my other nine children."

"Good-by," said Mrs. Goose, smoothing down her rumpled feathers.

"Peeeeep-peeeeep," said Little Duck, happily, running off behind his mother.

## Mrs. Goose's Supper

Mrs. Goose plop-plopped over to Mr. Gobbler's Grocery. She wanted to buy something good for supper.

On a shelf half-way up the wall, her black eyes spied some fat cheeses.

"Are those cheeses nice and fresh?" she asked Mr. Gobbler.

"Oh, very, very, very," Mr. Gobbler told her. "They just came in this morning."

"I'll take one," said Mrs. Goose. "It will be nice for my supper; just what I wanted."

So Mr. Gobbler hopped up on a chair, and lifted the plate of cheeses down with his bill.

Billy Squirrel, who worked in the grocery, put a little cheese cake in a box package for Mrs. Goose, and tied it up with a pink string.

"Thank you, good morning," said Mrs. Goose. And she plopped home, feeling very happy and hungry, and shaking her tail.

She untied her cheese cake and put it on her table. She got hungrier and hungrier. "I wish it was supper-time," she kept saying to herself.

At last she took a plate and spoon from the cupboard, and put them on the table. She said, "There; it is supper-time, right now." She sat down in her little kitchen chair and ate the cheese cake up.

"After that—after supper, time for bed, of course," said Mrs. Goose, quite forgetting that the morning sun was streaming in her little window.

She washed her plate and spoon, put on her long gray nightgown and her ruffly nightcap, and got into bed.

"After supper, time for bed," sighed Mrs. Goose, as she shut her eyes.

Very soon after that, Mrs. Squirrel came over to borrow a cup of sugar for her pie. She walked right into Mrs. Goose's house, for she often came in without knocking. She patted in softly; her squirrel feet made just a little skitter-scratch on the floor.

When she saw Mrs. Goose lying in bed with her eyes closed under her little ruffly nightcap,

she stopped short and stared at the sleeping sight.

"She must be sick!" she said. She tiptoed over to the bed and looked closer. "She has her night-gown on—" said Mrs. Squirrel to herself, whispering and worried. "She must be sick. She has undressed and gone to bed."

Mrs. Squirrel tiptoed out of the door. Three-Ducks were walking along the road, going down to the pond for a swim.

"Oh, Three-Ducks!" called Mrs. Squirrel, "come and see what the matter is. Mrs. Goose is in bed. She must be sick. Please come!"

So Three-Ducks waddled in. They looked at Mrs. Goose with their little bright black eyes. They saw her lying in bed with her long neck stretched out on the pillow, and her eyes shut tight, and her yellow bill open.

"Yes, she must be sick," said Three-Ducks. "She has put herself to bed in the daytime."

"We'd better make some catnip tea," said Mrs. Squirrel, "right away quick. Then we'll have it ready to pour down her throat the minute she opens her eyes. That will make her feel better." She rushed out into Mrs. Goose's tiny garden and picked some catnip. She traipsed around the kitchen and made the tea. Three-Ducks helped her.

"Now we'll take that tin cup," said Mrs. Squirrel, tying Mrs. Goose's apron around her brown fur self, "and we'll pour the tea in it. It can be cooling a little, till she wakes up."

She jumped on a chair to reach the cup. But,

oh, her foot slipped! The chair and the cup and Mrs. Squirrel all fell down with a whack and a clatter and a plop.

Mrs. Goose sat up in bed quickly. "What is the matter?" she asked. "What is going on, here in my house?"

"There, don't worry," said Mrs. Squirrel; "just be quiet." She quickly poured some tea into a china cup; she dashed some cold water into it to cool it; she rushed over to Mrs. Goose, and before the sleepy bird lady knew what she was about, Mrs. Squirrel had poured tea down her bill. Some of it spilled on her long gray nightgown and the bedclothes.

"Just drink this," Mrs. Squirrel kept telling her. "Soon you'll be all right."

"But I *am* all right!" Mrs. Goose spluttered. "I don't want any tea. Why, I've just had my supper!"

"Supper?" asked Mrs. Squirrel and Three-Ducks all together. "Why, it's only noon! See, the sun is high."

Mrs. Goose got out of bed and trailed her long gray nightgown over to the window. She looked up at the sky, turning her neck this way and that. "Why, so it *is* high," she said. "I bought a cheese cake for my supper. I got to thinking about supper, supper, supper. It is supper-time right away, I told myself; and I ate the cheese cake. Then, after supper, it was time to go to bed, wasn't it? I always go to bed after supper. So there I went."

Mrs. Squirrel and Three-Ducks began to laugh and laugh. "Why, you can't make it supper-time just by thinking it is," they told her. "You must look at your clock!" And they laughed some more.

"We thought you were sick!" quacked Three Ducks. "You should have seen yourself—in bed like that—with your bill open and your eyes shut and your nightcap on!"

"Well, my nightcap's on, now," said Mrs. Goose, "and I felt very cozy indeed, in bed, after my cheese cake. I think I'll go back there right now." And she trailed her long gray nightgown over the floor, and got back into bed again.

"Well, good night, then," said Three-Ducks. "Good noon, we mean." And they walked out of her house.

"Be sure and wake up when it gets dark,"

said Mrs. Squirrel, and she walked out too.

Outside, they laughed some more. But Mrs. Goose did not hear them. She had gone to sleep again, with her long neck stretched out on the pillow.

## THE JACK-O'-LANTERN GHOST

Mrs. Goose was passing by Mr. Gobbler's Grocery one late October day. She put down her big brown shopping-bag and stared at the things she saw in the window.

"What a lot of pumpkins," she said to herself. "I must go in and ask Mr. Gobbler why he has such a lot of pumpkins in piles like that."

So in she plop-plopped. Mr. Gobbler was tying up a bag of pink sugar, and when he saw Mrs. Goose, he said, "Good morning. Look out there, please; you are knocking over my onions."

"Oh, dear," said Mrs. Goose, "so I am. I didn't see them at all."

"Never mind," said Mr. Gobbler kindly. "What can I do for you?"

"I came to ask you," said Mrs. Goose, "why you have so many little pumpkins in the window."

"Because tonight is Hallowe'en," he told her. "You scoop out the middle of the pumpkins and cut faces in them. You put a candle in, and there, you have a Jack-o'-lantern."

"Oh, is that the way they make a Jack-o'-lantern?" asked Mrs. Goose. "I thought they grew in gardens. I will buy one of those little pumpkins, Mr. Gobbler."

So Mr. Gobbler selected a very round and ripe pumpkin for Mrs. Goose, and she hurried home with it, forgetting her shopping-bag. She had to go back for the bag, and she knocked the onions over again.

"Oh, I am so sorry," said Mrs. Goose, as she picked up the onions and put them by mistake with the oranges.

When at last she was at home in her little kitchen, she decided to go right to work making the Jack-o'-lantern. She cut a great jagged mouth and two squinty eyes; made a round nose. She ate a lot of pumpkin seeds and a great deal of the stringy, yellow pumpkin insides: so much that she felt a little too full and had to go and lie down on the bed, with her eyes shut and her feet sticking up and her wings spread out. She took a long nap, and when she got up she made some jelly, and drove the bumblebees out of her garden.

"Now," she said, "it is time for supper. It is beginning to get dark. I shall have only a glass of jelly for supper, because I must have time to dress myself up like a ghost and take my Jack-o'-lantern and go around scaring people."

So she found an old bed sheet and tied it around her middle, with the top over her head and the long ends trailing behind. "Now," she said, "when I have the lantern lit, the fun will begin. I wonder if I left room enough inside for the candle? I had better stick my head in and see."

So she jammed her goosie head through the Jack-o'-lantern's mouth. It was a tight squeeze, and the inside of the pumpkin was very damp and unpleasant. When she tried to pull her head out again, she could not. There she was, with the little round pumpkin on the top of her neck.

"Oh, goodness me," thought Mrs. Goose, "what shall I do? I can't see. I can't get loose." She shook her head. She flapped her wings. She ran around and around in her little room, knocking into chairs and making a great fuss. The ends of the sheet trailed about her legs and tripped her. After a while Mrs. Goose turned the pumpkin around a bit, so that she saw through one of the squinty Jack-o'-lantern eyes. Then she opened the door and rushed out into the darkness, calling, in a very stuffed-up way, because her bill was half shut and she could not talk very well: "Oh-come-quick-and-help-me-out-I-am-stuck-inside-this-pumpkin." But it sounded only like a lot of foolishness, and no one heard her at all, anyway.

Mrs. Goose ran to Mrs. Squirrel's house, with the sheet blowing around her legs and the pumpkin bobbing on her head. She looked through the window. There were Mr. Pig and Three-Ducks, sitting at Mrs. Squirrel's little blue painted table, and eating biscuits and honey with her. "Good!" thought Mrs. Goose, and she opened the door and rushed right in, so glad they were there to help her. But when they saw this queer, queer creature come so suddenly into the room, they jumped up from their chairs and quacked and squealed and grunted.

"Catch it, catch it!" shouted Mrs. Squirrel. "Shut it in the kitchen closet!"

"What is it, anyway?" chattered Three-Ducks, flying up, all three, on the clock shelf.

"A ghost with a pumpkin head," Mr. Pig told

them, and he seized a broom, and whacked Mrs. Goose hard, right where her tail was. She tried to tell him, "Don't! It is just your friend, Mrs. Goose!" But the only noise that came out was a thick whisper coming through the pumpkin, and before she knew it, she was shut into Mrs. Squirrel's kitchen closet, tight, with all the tin pans, the kettles, the floor cleaner and the mop. Then she heard Mr. Pig say through the door:

"Now I have it shut up, whatever it is. I have saved our lives."

They all went back and began to eat again. She could hear Mr. Pig and Mrs. Squirrel and Three-Ducks scraping their dishes with their spoons. She tried to call out again, but she could not. She began thumping her pumpkin head against the kettles that hung on the wall inside the dark closet, and of course that made a loud rattly noise.

"Keep still," called Mr. Pig. "When I get through eating, I shall come and chase you out where you belong."

So Mrs. Goose was still. But after a while, she forgot what Mr. Pig had said, and made a great bang again.

"Now," said Mr. Pig, "I am coming to fix you."

He came thumping over and opened the door. Mrs. Squirrel and Three-Ducks huddled in the corner. Mr. Pig held his broom high, and whacked Mrs. Goose's pumpkin head, a great hard whack!

"There you are," he said. "You bad old fat ghost!"

The pumpkin broke in two, and showed Mrs. Goose's head, with her eyes shut.

"Why, it's Mrs. Goose!" quacked Three-Ducks.

"It's Mrs. Goose!" chattered Mrs. Squirrel.

Mrs. Goose opened her eyes and looked around. Mr. Pig held the door wide, and she walked out of the closet, trailing her sheet behind her.

"Oh, dear!" she began to cry. "Oh, dear! I was planning to scare you a little for Hallowe'en. Then I got that Jack-o'-lantern tight on my poor head, and I had to give up my plans. But I did so want to help you to celebrate Hallowe'en."

"But you did scare us; indeed you did," said Mrs. Squirrel.

"We thought you were a ghost," said Mr. Pig.

"Why, we even shut you up in the closet," said Three-Ducks, "because we were so afraid of you!" Then they all began to laugh, even Mrs. Goose.

"It must have been very horrid," said Mrs. Squirrel, "squeezed into the closet like that and whacked. There now, sit down and have some supper, you poor thing, and when you have finished, we'll all put on sheets and go around scaring our animal friends. Shall we?"

"I think I've had enough Hallowe'en," said Mrs. Goose, gulping down a biscuit.

"You won't feel that way after you've eaten," Mr. Pig told her. "You'll be all right."

And she was. They went all around, tapping at windows and making queer noises and having a great deal of fun. They had some raisin cake at Three-Ducks' house, and then they took Mrs. Goose home.

"Thank you," she said as she unlocked the door. "But what have I forgotten? When I started out, I'm sure I had something that I haven't now."

"The Jack-o'-lantern, Mrs. Goose," they told her. "The Jack-o'-lantern on your head."

"Oh, yes, that was it," she said. "Well, I don't want *that*, I'm sure. I had a much better time without it." And she went in and went to bed, all wrapped up in her ghost sheet for a nightgown.

## One-Duck and Two-Ducks

One day when Mrs. Goose was making a hot pot-pie for her breakfast in her cozy kitchen, she heard a quacking by her window. She looked out, and there were—Two-Ducks! Not Three-Ducks—who always were together—but just Two-Ducks. Mrs. Goose was very surprised. She could not believe her black eyes. She opened the window quickly, and stuck her head out.

"What is the matter?" she asked.

"Oh, we've lost one of us!" said Two-Ducks. "We were sleeping at the edge of the pond, and one of us got frozen in!"

"Then," said Mrs. Goose, "I must take my

hot teakettle and we will go to the edge of the pond and pour hot water on the ice."

"Yes, yes," quacked Two-Ducks, thinking this was very clever of Mrs. Goose.

So she hurried out of her house with the steaming kettle, and Two-Ducks came along behind her, crying.

When they reached the edge of the pond, sure enough, there was One-Duck, frozen in the ice. His eyes were shut and he looked very cold and miserable.

"*Quick,* quack; *quick,* quack," he said, when he saw them coming. "Please get me out."

"That is just what we are going to do," said Mrs. Goose. "See, I have the hot teakettle."

"Oh, but that will be too hot! It will burn me," cried One-Duck.

"Quack, quack," said Two-Ducks. "It will burn him."

"So it will," said Mrs. Goose, and set the kettle down. "I hadn't thought of that. Then we must wait for the water to cool."

"That's so," quacked Two-Ducks, sitting down on the ice. Mrs. Goose sat down there, too. They all waited.

After a while Mrs. Goose said: "Now the water is cool."

"But if it is cool, it will not melt the ice," said Two-Ducks. "We should have thought of that before."

"Let me try it and see," said Mrs. Goose, pouring water all around One-Duck. But of course it did not melt the ice. It only made One-Duck wet. He opened his eyes and quacked: "You have only made things worse! *Quick,* quack, get an ax! You will have to chop me out."

"That's a good idea; but who has an ax?" asked Two-Ducks, blinking.

"Mr. Pop-Rabbit has an ax," said Mrs. Goose. "And I will go and ask him for it."

"Please sit down by me and wait," said One-Duck to Two-Ducks. "I am very lonesome without you."

So Two-Ducks sat down on the ice beside One-Duck, and Mrs. Goose hurried off to Mr. Pop-Rabbit's.

After a while they saw her coming back with the ax. "Oh, that looks dangerous!" they quacked. "You will chop in the wrong place, and One-Duck will be hurt."

"No, I will not," said Mrs. Goose. "Get up,

Two-Ducks, so that I can see better. You are all so close together."

But when Two-Ducks tried to rise from the ice beside their brother they found that they could not move!

"The water you poured on the ice has frozen, and now we are *all* stuck in the ice," they quacked.

"What a time of it we are having!" cried Mrs. Goose. "What shall I do? I must get you out."

"Try pulling us," said One-Duck, without opening his eyes.

So Mrs. Goose took hold of his tail, and pulled, but he quacked: "No, no; stop that! You hurt me."

Poor Mrs. Goose sat down on the ice beside them again and said: "Oh, dear; I don't know what to do."

Now, all this time the sun was coming out from under the clouds. It shone right down on the edge of the pond and warmed the backs of Three-Ducks and Mrs. Goose, sitting there so miserably.

Then Mrs. Goose jumped up and said: "Well, if you must stay here, I'll stay with you. But I am going home to get my breakfast pot-pie, and we'll eat it together. That will make us all feel better."

"All right, Mrs. Goose," said Three-Ducks; "but don't be long."

So Mrs. Goose plopped home, and the dreary cold day had cleared up; the sun shone right down on her back. When she got near her house she saw smoke coming out of her kitchen window.

"Oh, my house is on fire! My house is on fire!" she cried out loud.

When she opened the door there was a dreadful smell of something burning. Then she knew that it was her breakfast pot-pie, left in the oven.

Sure enough, when she rushed to look, there was just a mess of cinders and a strong black smoke.

"Well, I must make another one, then," said Mrs. Goose, and she set right to work. When the pie was done, the sun was well up over the tops of the trees. Mrs. Goose unbuttoned her coat, she got so warm hurrying down to the edge of the pond with the pot-pie.

"Three-Ducks—Three-Ducks—" she called. "I have our breakfast!"

But Three-Ducks were not there. There was

just a sloshy, melted place where they had been.

"Now, I wonder how they got loose?" thought Mrs. Goose. "And here I am, all alone with my pot-pie. I don't know what to do. I'll go over to the edge of the little wood and sit on a stump and think."

So she did. The sun shone down on her, so

warm that she had to take off her coat. Very soon she felt simply weak with being so hot and so hungry, and lay down on the ground with her feet sticking up into the air and went to sleep. She slept till she felt herself being poked with a stick; very slowly she opened one black eye and took a peek. There were Three-Ducks looking at her over a log, and all laughing in a row!

"Get up!" they said. "You look perfectly crazy, lying there on the ground like that. Put on your coat and tie your scarf around your long goosie neck—we're going over to our house for some hot corn soup. We've been looking for you everywhere; Black Cat said he saw you go into the woods, and so we found you. Do hurry!"

"All right," said Mrs. Goose, scrambling up. "I'll take my pot-pie and heat it up in your ice-box. Ice-box? Ice-box. That makes me think of something. How did you get away from the ice, Three-Ducks?"

"Oh, we melted loose, of course," said Three-Ducks. "Spring's just around the corner."

"Well, I'm glad you're together again," said Mrs. Goose, plopping along behind them. "One-Duck and Two-Ducks makes Three-Ducks."

## Mrs. Goose's Vacation Trip

It was a bright summer day, and there sat Mrs. Goose on the porch of her little house. Suddenly she said to herself, "I'm going on a trip. I'm going to have a little vacation. Why, I just stay here, day after day, month after month, always right in my little house, and I never see anything of the world. The farthest I have been for a long time is Mr. Gobbler's Grocery. I'm going in to pack, right now."

So into the house she flew. She found a big, blue laundry bag, and set about filling it with things. Her best red shoes, her soap and wash-cloth and long gray nightgown and nightcap, her blue and lavender party dress, a candle and a dipper and two big books. "And I might be hungry," said Mrs. Goose; "there's bread and raisin cake and one cold muffin in the bread-box—" So she squeezed the bread-box, with all the things in it, right into the bag and pulled the strings up tight.

Then she put on her red shawl and her hat with the parsley on it, took her umbrella out of the dark hall closet, went out of the door and turned the key in the lock.

"Dear me, dear me," laughed Mrs. Goose to herself as she stood on the porch. "I'm going to take a vacation trip, and I forgot to get the money to buy my ticket with!" She dashed back into her little house and took silver pieces out of the long black stocking where she kept them. Then she was ready to start again. "No one can say that *I* forget things," Mrs. Goose laughed to herself.

Mrs. Squirrel was sweeping off the porch of her little house. "Why, hello, Mrs. Goose," she said, when she saw her neighbor coming out of her door looking very fixed up and in a hurry. "Where are *you* going?"

"I'm going on a vacation trip," Mrs. Goose told her. "I'm tired of just staying home."

"Well, well!" Mrs. Squirrel was very surprised. "But *where* are you going?"

"Oh, I don't know yet. I'll just take the train somewhere."

"But don't you know *where?*"

"Of course not. I'll decide that when I get to the station. It's too early yet to tell," said Mrs. Goose, shaking her tail.

Mrs. Squirrel dropped her broom, she was so astonished. "But I never heard of any one taking a trip without knowing where she was going!" she told Mrs. Goose. "Don't you know—?"

But Mrs. Goose was quite far down the street by that time, almost as far as Blue Brook. Three-Ducks were there, kicking their yellow feet in the water.

"Hello!" they quacked. "What under the sun are you up to? What are you doing with that big blue laundry bag? Are you going to do your washing here in the brook?"

"It's not a laundry bag—it's a traveling-bag," said Mrs. Goose. "I'm going on a little summer vacation trip—that's where I'm going." She marched right along, holding her head up high on her long white neck.

"But where?"

"I don't *know* yet," Mrs. Goose told them rather crossly. "I haven't decided." She was a little vexed and snappish at being talked to so much about her trip, so she planned to take the little road through Willow Woods. "I am sure I can find the Animaltown station from there—I know where the road comes out—I think—" she told herself proudly. "And if I go through the woods, I won't meet any of my foolish friends asking where I am going."

So she went on. The bag with the bread-box in it got very heavy. Mrs. Goose had a thought. "I can make the box lighter by eating the things there are in it!" So she sat down on an old stump and gobbled the bread and the cold muffin and the raisin cake; it was really more than she wanted, but she finished them all. Then she stuffed the bread-box back into the blue bag again, with just the pieces of money rattling around in it. "That was very bright of me," said Mrs. Goose, "not to eat the money, too."

There was a whirring noise in the tree-tops over her head. There was Old Lady Owl.

"Youuuuuuuuu!" she said, blinking her great eyes at Mrs. Goose. "What are you going to dooooooooo?"

"I'm going on a vacation trip," said Mrs. Goose.

"But where are you going toooooooooo?"

"I don't KNOW yet!" flapped Mrs. Goose, feeling very cross indeed that she couldn't be let alone about her trip, even in the Wild Woods.

Old Lady Owl blinked at her, and Mrs. Goose thought she heard her laughing, soft, queer, feathery laughter. But Mrs. Goose walked on. And after a little while she came out of the woods.

"That's very funny," she said, stretching her long neck this way and that, "but I don't see the Animaltown Railroad Station. I expected it to be right here. And I wanted to buy my ticket— Well, I'll just go right on. Over there is the train track. If I keep walking, I'll surely come to the station."

So she went along and along, under the hot June sun, right on the track. Soon she heard a tooting. There came the Animaltown train: the engineer was a goat, and he was leaning way out of the window, with his long beard blowing in the wind. He was very excited when he saw Mrs. Goose walking on the railroad track!

But Mrs. Goose hopped off, just in time. The train whizzed by, and all the animal people waved to her out of the window.

"Too bad, too bad that I missed that train," sighed Mrs. Goose. "Well, never mind. I'll get the next one. I'll buy a ticket just as soon as I get to the station."

So she walked and she walked and she walked. She began to be hungry again, and she wished that she had not eaten up all the things in her bread-box. Then, after a little while, she saw the roof of a little red station around the bend.

"Funny—that doesn't look like Animaltown," thought Mrs. Goose, but she plop-plopped to the station and looked in the window. There was an old badger man sitting at the ticket-window.

"Hello," said Mrs. Goose. "What station is this?"

"Place-in-the-Woods," said the badger man.

"Hmmmmm, that's funny. I didn't expect to be *here,* at all. Well, I've come to buy a ticket."

"A ticket to where, madam?" asked the badger man.

"I haven't decided yet," Mrs. Goose told him. "Will you please tell me some of the places I could go to?"

The badger man blinked at her. "Deer Pond," he said. "Skunk River."

"Deer Pond sounds too wet," said Mrs. Goose, "and I don't care for skunks. What other places are there?"

"Well, there's High Mountain, where the Bears live."

"Oh, that wouldn't do at all! I don't care for bears, either. Where else could I go?"

"There's Wolf Cave," grunted the badger man. Mrs. Goose made a soft hissing noise and shut her eyes. "I simply *hate* wolves," she shuddered. "Isn't there some other place?"

"Well, there's Animaltown, twenty-five scrambles back. The train just came from there."

"Why that's where I *live!*" Mrs. Goose was delighted. "And it's such a nice place: such a good, safe little town, no wolves or bears—and all my friends live there. Give me a ticket to Animaltown, please."

"The train won't be back till two winks after sundown," said the badger man.

"That's all right. I'll just sit here in your station and wait." And Mrs. Goose shut her black eyes, stretched her long neck over the blue laundry bag, and was fast asleep in no time.

* * * * * * *

She slept and she slept till she felt a poking on her wing. "It's two winks after sundown—here comes the train—" The badger man stood over her, showing all his teeth. Mrs. Goose didn't like the way he looked. She hated teeth when they showed like that. She sprang up and rushed to the little door. "Here's your bag, madam!" The badger man came after her.

"Thank you," said Mrs. Goose, and stuffed it under her wing.

The train tooted, came around the bend, and stopped. Mrs. Goose was so excited that she tried to hop up and get in a window, but the badger man pushed her from behind, very firmly, up the train steps. Then she was safe inside the car. "Good-by," she called. "I've had a very nice time, sleeping in your station!"

* * * * * * *

When the fox conductor called "Animaltown!" Mrs. Goose hurried down the train steps. She forgot her bag; one of the passengers threw it at her from a window. It whacked her on the head and knocked her hat off. Mrs. Goose blinked, said "What was THAT?" picked up her hat, picked up the bag, said "Oh!"—and started along the little road that led to her house.

There were Three-Ducks in Blue Brook again, having their evening swim. "Hello, where did you go to?" they asked her.

"I didn't go anywhere," Mrs. Goose told them. "I just came back to Animaltown."

Three-Ducks stared at her. Mrs. Squirrel came by, with her knitting.

"Hello," she said. "Here you are, with your big blue bag and all. Do you know, I was a little worried about you. You didn't seem to know where you were going. Well, did you really go away?"

"Oh, no," said Mrs. Goose. "I didn't go

away, at all. I just came *back*." And she went plop-plopping down the road.

"Now, what does she mean by *that?*" Mrs. Squirrel asked Three-Ducks.

"Quack, quack, quack," said Three-Ducks. "We don't know. We asked her, too, and she said the same thing to us."

## Mrs. Goose's Wild Christmas

One morning in December when Mrs. Goose went to her front door, there was a letter for her. It was written on birch-bark paper, and tied around with green grass ribbon.

Mrs. Goose was so excited that her wings fluttered and trembled. She opened the envelope, sat down in her little rocking-chair, and put on her glasses.

The letter was printed in queer, green, wiggly letters. It said:

"Dear Mrs. Goose,

Please come and spend Christmas with me in my river home. I will fly by for you at five o'clock on Christmas Eve. Be ready to fly up and fly away with me.

Your flying cousin,
MRS. WILD-GOOSE-OF-THE-MARSHES."

"My, there are a lot of 'flys' in that letter," said Mrs. Goose, blinking. She got up from her rocking-chair and said to herself, "I don't believe I know how to fly. I've been a tame goose for so long that I've forgotten."

She thought for a minute, and then she flapped her wings. "No, I haven't forgotten," she told herself.

Three-Ducks were coming over for a cup of hot clover tea at four o'clock. Mrs. Goose kept very busy till they came, tying up presents for her friends. Three yellow bow-ties for Three-Ducks, a nice new tail-comb for Mrs. Squirrel, and little currant cakes for Mr. Pig and the Pop-Rabbits and her other friends. "Don't open till Christmas," she wrote on them. "They can look at them when they have the big Animaltown Christmas Tree party," she planned. "But I won't be here!" Yes, she had decided to spend Christmas with her wild marsh cousin.

At four o'clock, she heard a quacking at the

door, and she ran to let Three-Ducks in. "It's getting very cold and blowy," they told her, as they marched over to the fire. "We think it's going to snow," they said, as they warmed their wings.

"I hope it won't snow on Christmas Eve at five o'clock," Mrs. Goose told them. "Because I am going away then."

"*Away?*" quacked Three-Ducks, looking at her.

"Yes, away; I am going to visit my cousin, Mrs. Wild-Goose," and she showed them the birch-bark letter.

"Oh, Mrs. Goose—you won't be here for Christmas—and our big Animaltown party," said Three-Ducks.

"No."

"Why—we'll miss you so much!"

"I'll miss you, too," said Mrs. Goose, getting the teapot.

"And you'll not like the way your cousin lives. She doesn't have a cozy home like yours! She sleeps in a wet river place."

Mrs. Goose poured the tea. "Yes, but she *is* my cousin," she told Three-Ducks. "Our mothers were sister geese. I have decided to go."

They drank their tea, and they talked some more about it, but Three-Ducks couldn't make Mrs. Goose change her mind. She was just determined to go on Christmas Eve; that was all there was about it.

On the day before Christmas, Mrs. Goose was very busy. She tied bright bunches of holly berries on her friends' presents. She packed a little bag with her long gray nightgown and funny white nightcap, and feather-brush. She swept her house and put it all in order. Then she put on her red shoes and her blue and lavender dress and bright red shawl and hat with parsley on it.

She looked at herself in the glass and said, "There I am. I look very handsome, really—I hope my cousin will be proud of me."

*Tap—tap—tap.* That was Three-Ducks at the door. They had come to see her off. *Scratch—scratch—scratch.* That was Mrs. Squirrel. Then came Mr. Pig and Mr. Gobbler and the Pop-Rabbits. It was very exciting, coming to see Mrs. Goose fly off—just like waiting to see a balloon go up, or something. "Do you *know* how to fly?" asked Mrs. Squirrel. "Yes, I know," answered Mrs. Goose.

They all went outside to watch for Mrs. Wild-Goose.

The wind made little scurry-tracks in the snow, and there were gray clouds scudding over.

"I wish she'd hurry," said Mrs. Goose, drawing her shawl closer around her. "I'm cold."

"I wish you'd change your mind," sighed Mrs. Squirrel. "I hate to think of your flying around loose in the sky somewhere. Don't go!!"

"Yes, I'm going," said Mrs. Goose, firmly.

"I don't believe her cousin is coming," Three-Ducks whispered. "It's five minutes past five already."

But just then there was a far away honking sound. In a minute, a wild goose came into sight. She came nearer and nearer. She flew over Mrs. Goose's chimney.

"There she is—good-by—" said Mrs. Goose, flapping her wings.

But there she stayed, right on the ground.

"Try again," said Three-Ducks.

She flapped and flapped, but she did not rise.

"Take off your clothes!" came a wild voice from the sky. "Throw off your bag! You are toooo heavy!" And there was a sound like laughter, cold laughter, with wind in it.

So. Mrs. Goose took off her dress, and her shawl, and her hat, and threw her bag down on the ground. She flapped her wings again, and up she rose, with a great noise. As she rose, she kicked off her red shoes. They fell down and

one of them whacked Mr. Pig on the nose.

"Good-by—Mrs. Goose—" Mr. Pig sneezed.

"Good-by," they all called.

"Good-by—" she answered them, as she rose higher and higher.

"There she goes, for her wild Christmas," said

Three-Ducks. "I hope she'll have a good time." They gulped hard in their throats, because they missed her already. "We'd better take her things into the house, and lock the door, just as she told us to, and put the key under the mat. There she flies—over the pine tree-tops. And there are going to be lots of presents for her at the Christmas party tomorrow—and she won't be here to get them. She said she'd open them when she got back."

"Maybe she won't *get* back," sighed Mrs. Squirrel. "Maybe we'll never see her again." And they all began to cry a little, feeling so sad on Christmas Eve at quarter past five o'clock.

At seven o'clock, when Three-Ducks came back from a little visit at Mrs. Squirrel's house, there was a light shining from Mrs. Goose's window.

"We must go and look in," they said. "Who could be there? Mrs. Goose is away. We must go and see."

So they plopped over and peeked in the window.

There was Mrs. Goose with her wrapper and white nightcap on, warming her wings before the fire.

*Tap-tap-tap* at the door went Three-Ducks, with excited bills. They were *so* glad!

"Shhhhhh!" said Mrs. Goose, as she let them in. "Yes, I'm back. (Whisper.) Yes, my wings are tired. (*Please* whisper!) For my wild cousin is here—she's in my bed, sleeping. She's come to spend Christmas with me."

"But we thought you were going to spend Christmas with *her!*"

"I did spend two hours with her," said Mrs. Goose. "That was long enough. Yes, you were right, Three-Ducks. Her house is very cold, right by the river. Just frozen rattly reeds, lumps of ice, and wind blowing your feathers this way and that. One of my best tail feathers blew right out! She had a few wintergreen berries stuck around; we ate those. 'This is our Christmas dinner, really,' said my cousin. 'We'll have it today, instead of tomorrow. We'll spend Christmas flying, my tame cousin. You need practice. You fly very badly. We'll go far over those snow-covered hills.' "

"How cold and unpleasant," shivered Three-Ducks. "What did you say?"

"I said—'Now I've had a sort of a Christmas with you—a nice berry meal—please come back to my house with me, and see what Christmas there is like. We give presents to each other; we have a party and lots of dancing and laughing, and try to make each other happy and full of pleasant feelings.' And do you know—she had never heard of a party in a house beside a fire. She didn't know about giving presents! Awfully wild, I think. Well, I talked and talked, and after a while she said she would come."

"And she's here now—sleeping in your bed?" asked Three-Ducks. "Oh, do let us have a peek at her, please."

"Will you be very quiet? Will you put your feet down softly, and not quack?"

"Oh, yes; yes."

So Mrs. Goose lit a candle, and they stepped softly to the bedroom. She held the light up high, so they could see better.

But there was no one in the bed!

The covers were thrown back, as though some one had got out quickly, and there was one long feather on the blanket.

"Why—she's *gone,*" said Mrs. Goose, looking at the open window.

"She's flown away. You can't be wild, and she can't be tame," said Three-Ducks, wisely.

"Our mothers were sister geese," Mrs. Goose told them. "But *we* don't seem to belong in the same family."

"And you'll be here for the Christmas party, after all," laughed Three-Ducks.

* * * * * * *

And they had the happiest Christmas that they had ever had. Ragtag and Bobtail and Billy Squirrel and all the other animal children had some jolly little toys, and all the grown-up animals had great fun opening their own presents. They sang animal songs, and played games, and the refreshments were delicious. The tree was trimmed with little balls of cotton, strings of pink pop-corn, and a few stars and candles.

Mrs. Goose was so happy that she got all

mixed up: she dropped nuts into her tea instead of lemon, said "Happy birthday" to Mr. Pig instead of "Merry Christmas," and when it was time to go home, she put her rubbers on her wings instead of on her feet. But no one cared, they were so glad to see her back again. "And you won't fly away again, will you?" Three-Ducks asked her.

And she said, "No. One wild Christmas is enough for me. Animaltown is where *I* belong, forever and ever!"

And now close the book, because this is

THE END